HORSES SET I

Arabian Horses

BreAnn Rumsch
ABDO Publishing Company

visit us at
www.abdopublishing.com

Published by ABDO Publishing Company, 8000 West 78th Street, Edina, Minnesota 55439. Copyright © 2011 by Abdo Consulting Group, Inc. International copyrights reserved in all countries. No part of this book may be reproduced in any form without written permission from the publisher. The Checkerboard Library™ is a trademark and logo of ABDO Publishing Company.

Printed in the United States of America, North Mankato, Minnesota.
042010
092010

 PRINTED ON RECYCLED PAPER

Cover Photo: Alamy
Interior Photos: Alamy p. 21; AP Images pp. 9, 12; iStockphoto pp. 7, 11, 19;
    Jupiter Images p. 13; Photolibrary pp. 5, 15, 17

Editor: Heidi M.D. Elston
Art Direction & Cover Design: Neil Klinepier

Library of Congress Cataloging-in-Publication Data

Rumsch, BreAnn, 1981-
 Arabian horses / BreAnn Rumsch.
     p. cm. -- (Horses)
 Includes index.
 ISBN 978-1-61613-418-1
 1. Arabian horse--Juvenile literature. I. Title.

SF293.A8R86 2011
636.1'12--dc22

                    2010009572

CONTENTS

WHERE ARABIANS CAME FROM

Horses are beautiful, spirited animals. Humans use these creatures for work, travel, and play. Horses also serve as close companions to humans.

These powerful mammals belong to the family **Equidae**. Their earliest ancestor was eohippus. This fox-sized creature lived about 60 million years ago. Since then, horses have developed into many **breeds**.

The Arabian is one of the oldest modern horse breeds. It first appeared more than 2,000 years ago. At that time, it was established on the Arabian Peninsula in the Middle East. Starting in the 1700s, the breed spread to Europe. Arabians were first bred in the United States in 1888.

Arabians are considered the origin of most modern horse breeds.

What Arabians Look Like

The Arabian horse is considered unmatched in its beauty. Its head is unmistakable. The wide-set eyes are large and bulging. A broad forehead tapers to a narrow **muzzle** with large nostrils. From the side, the face appears to scoop in above the nose.

A high, arched neck is another mark of an Arabian. The horse has a long, silky mane and tail. The tail is held high.

Arabian horses weigh an average of 800 to 1,000 pounds (360 to 450 kg). They stand about 15 hands high. Each hand equals four inches (10 cm). This measurement is taken from the ground up to the horse's **withers**.

An Arabian's face shape is often described as dished.

WHAT MAKES ARABIANS SPECIAL

The deserts of the Middle East are windy, dry, and vast. Over time, Arabian horses adapted to these harsh conditions. They grew into horses known for their speed and strength.

Today, Arabians compete in many sports. These include racing and endurance riding. No other **breed** can run long distances like the Arabian.

In addition to its abilities, the Arabian has a good disposition. It is gentle, affectionate, and loves to be around people. The Arabian is also courageous and loyal.

Today, Arabian horses are well loved. Many other horses are **bred** with Arabians to improve their speed, endurance, and spirit. For example, Arabians helped to develop the Thoroughbred racehorse.

Arabians make good friends. They are known to act more like pets than other horse breeds.

COLOR

Arabians are solid-colored horses. They can be gray, bay, chestnut, black, or roan. Gray is the most popular color. Gray horses usually turn white with age.

A bay horse has a light to dark reddish brown coat with black points. Points are the horse's legs, mane, and tail. A horse with a brown coat and no black points is a chestnut.

Black horses have black coats and points. Roan horses have white hairs mixed with bay, chestnut, or black hairs. Roan coloring is rare among Arabians.

Arabians can have white markings on the head and the legs. Head markings include a **bald face**, a star, a stripe, a **blaze**, and a **snip**. Leg markings may be a **coronet**, a sock, or a stocking.

Daily grooming helps keep your Arabian's coat healthy and clean. Owners need a rubber currycomb to remove dirt from the horse's coat. A body brush cleans the Arabian's skin. Owners should use sponges to clean the horse's face and under its tail.

Whatever their color, all Arabians are beautiful animals.

CARE

An Arabian horse should have a comfortable place to live. A stabled Arabian needs its own stall

Arabians should have their teeth checked once a year.

with plenty of fresh air. Owners should also provide clean bedding.

A veterinarian will need to examine your Arabian at least once a year. He or she can give regular **vaccines** and **deworm** the horse.

With age, your horse's teeth may become uneven and sharp. This can cause chewing problems or mouth injuries. The veterinarian can file down the teeth until they are even. This is called floating.

Much like fingernails, horse hooves continue to grow throughout a horse's life. Trimming your horse's hooves helps prevent problems from uneven wear. Horseshoes protect the Arabian's hooves from chipping or cracking.

You can remove dirt and stones from your horse's hooves with a hoof pick. This will prevent discomfort.

13

FEEDING

Most owners feed their Arabians twice each day. The amount and type of food a horse needs depends on several factors. These include size, age, and amount of exercise.

All Arabian horses eat hay. The most popular kinds are timothy hay and alfalfa. A horse that is not working should need only hay.

A working Arabian needs grain added to its diet. Oats, barley, and corn are most common. Hay and grain can be mixed together or fed separately.

Fresh water should always be available. Arabians may drink less water than other horses. But, no horse can survive more than a few days without it. Horses also need salt available for them to lick. This helps replace salt lost while sweating.

Bad hay can make your Arabian very ill. Only feed hay that is green and smells fresh and sweet.

THINGS ARABIANS NEED

Horse lovers know riding is a great way to enjoy an Arabian. An Arabian's riding equipment is called tack. Tack should fit well to prevent pain or injury to the horse.

Riders can choose from two types of saddles. The English saddle is small and light. It is used for jumping and racing. The Western saddle is larger and has a **horn**. It is used for long-distance riding and ranching.

A saddle pad or blanket rests underneath the saddle. It absorbs sweat and helps the saddle stay in place. Stirrups attach to the sides of the saddle. The rider places his or her feet in them.

A bridle allows the rider to control the horse. Three parts make up the bridle. The headstall goes over the horse's head and attaches to the bit. The bit sits in the horse's mouth. It attaches to the reins, which the rider holds.

Owners should clean their Arabian's tack after every ride. This protects the horse's skin and extends the tack's life.

How Arabians Grow

A baby horse is called a foal. An adult female is called a mare. A **breeding** male is called a stallion. After mating, a mare is **pregnant** for about 11 months.

An Arabian foal may take its first wobbly steps a few minutes after birth. Within the first hour, it will start drinking its mother's milk. A foal can trot and gallop beside its mother in about 24 hours.

An Arabian foal is **weaned** when it is four or five months old. Then, it spends its time growing and playing with other young horses. They learn how to jump, run, and balance themselves.

Healthy Arabians should live at least 20 years. Some have been known to survive more than 30 years.

About a week after birth, a foal's milk teeth begin to appear. These are replaced by permanent teeth as the horse ages.

TRAINING

Arabian horses are intelligent and eager to please. In fact, they learn more quickly than other horse **breeds**.

However, training an Arabian requires skill and patience. Trainers teach Arabians by repeating words and certain hand and leg movements. The horse learns to recognize these commands.

Before this training begins, an Arabian foal must learn to wear some of its tack. First, the foal adjusts to a head collar called a halter. As it grows, the foal begins to accept handling from a person.

In its second year, the Arabian begins training on a lunge line. The horse also learns to wear a bit. Next, the horse learns to wear a saddle. But, an Arabian should not be ridden until it is at least two and a half years old.

On a lunge line, a horse moves in a circle at different paces. The horse learns to follow its trainer's commands.

Properly trained Arabian horses can perform many sports or jobs. This beautiful **breed** is sure to stay popular with horse lovers for years to come!

GLOSSARY

bald face - a white, wide marking covering most of an animal's face.

blaze - a usually white, broad stripe down the center of an animal's face.

breed - a group of animals sharing the same ancestors and appearance. A breeder is a person who raises animals. Raising animals is often called breeding them.

coronet - a white marking on the band around the top of a horse's hoof.

deworm - to rid of worms.

Equidae (EEK-wuh-dee) - the scientific name for the family of mammals that includes horses, zebras, and donkeys.

horn - a part of a saddle around which a rope can be tied.

muzzle - an animal's nose and jaws.

pregnant - having one or more babies growing within the body.

snip - a white marking between a horse's nostrils.

vaccine (vak-SEEN) - a shot given to prevent illness or disease.

wean - to accustom an animal to eating food other than its mother's milk.

withers - the highest part of a horse's or other animal's back.

WEB SITES

To learn more about Arabian horses, visit ABDO Publishing Company on the World Wide Web at **www.abdopublishing.com**. Web sites about Arabians are featured on our Book Links page. These links are routinely monitored and updated to provide the most current information available.

INDEX